Lulu's Back In Town

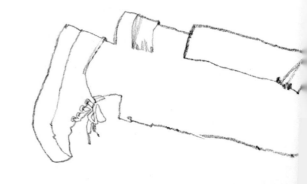

Lulu's Back In Town

story by Leigh Dean

pictures by Ted Coconis

Funk & Wagnalls, New York

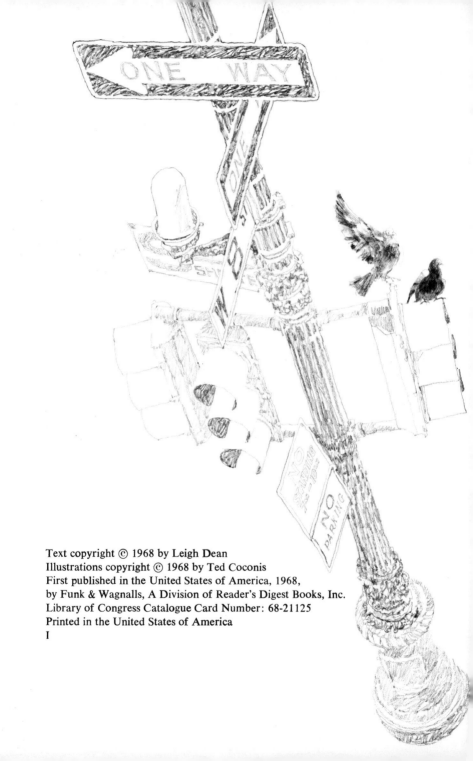

Text copyright © 1968 by Leigh Dean
Illustrations copyright © 1968 by Ted Coconis
First published in the United States of America, 1968,
by Funk & Wagnalls, A Division of Reader's Digest Books, Inc.
Library of Congress Catalogue Card Number: 68-21125
Printed in the United States of America
I

For my mother
who raised a lulu

It was Sunday afternoon on Eighth Street—and very quiet. Just another hot, summer Sunday. Up and down the block people sat on their cement stoops or leaned out windows or stood in shady doorways, fanning themselves.

Most of the kids were at the public pool. But not the Eighth Street gang. The Eighth Street gang was a small gang; it had only six members. There were Melvin Jones, Tory Aiken, Steve Cohen, Gus Lipswich, Edgar Jackson and Lulu O'Rourke. They

were all in the same grade; in September, they would all be in Grade 4 at P.S. 41.

But now it was vacation time and August and four of the six members were sitting around on melon crates outside Louie's Fruit Stand, reading.

"It sure is dead," said Tory, brushing a fly off his face.

"Yeah," said Melvin and turned the page of his *Batman* comic.

"My glasses keep fogging up," said Edgar. "Every time I breathe through my mouth, they fog up."

"Why don't you breathe through your nose," said Steve.

"Can't," said Edgar. And everyone went back to his reading—except Edgar. Edgar took off his steel-rimmed glasses, took out a crumpled kleenex from his pants pocket and began to give his glasses a slow, thorough cleaning. 'Melvin doesn't have to wear glasses. Melvin doesn't even have to take a bath,' he thought to himself while he polished the lenses. 'And another thing. How come I'm the only one who gets sunburned . . . except for Tory? And he's colored so it never shows. It isn't fair.'

"Hey," said Steve, "look who's coming!"

"It's only Gus," said Melvin.

"Yeah," said Tory, "but fat Gus only runs if it's somethin' important."

Gus ran and ran and finally puffed to a stop in front of Louie's Fruit Stand.

"Hi, Gus," said Melvin. "What's new?"

"Hi, Melvin. Hi, Tory. Hi, Steve. Hi, Edgar. Guess what?" said Gus, "Lulu's back in town."

"Great!" shouted the guys.

It had been a long slow summer ever since Lulu had gone away to camp. No matter what they planned, things just weren't as high without Lulu.

"Hey, remember when Lulu showed us how to raise crickets. . . ."

". . . on milkweed plants . . ."

". . . and we took our collection to science class . . ."

". . . and they all got loose!"

"Man," sighed Tory, "that was great!"

"When is she gonna call a meeting?" asked Steve.

"She didn't say," said Gus.

"How'd she look?" asked Steve.

"The same, only browner," said Gus.

"Let's split so we don't miss the message," said Tory.

10

"Right," said Steve, and got up to go. "Aren't you leaving?" he asked Melvin.

"In a while," said Melvin. "I want to finish this story."

The rest of the Eighth Street gang said "so long" and left Melvin and his pile of comic books and headed toward their homes.

After a while, Melvin closed the comic and thought about Lulu and those eyes of hers that could look at you so hard you knew she knew your most hidden secrets. Lulu was nine years old. And she was back in town.

That evening Lulu sent out a message along the clothesline network high above the city streets.

E.S.G.
MEET AT LOUIE'S TOMORROW
8 A.M. PREPARE FOR A LONG TRIP
LULU

At exactly 8 a.m., the Eighth Street gang assembled. And there was Lulu, lean, straw-haired, and freckly with her hands on her hips, waiting.

11

"Hi, Lulu."

"Hi, gang," said Lulu, and before they could start asking her a lot of questions about her trip, she began roll call. "Melvin, did you bring green soap and bandaids?"

"Right here," said Melvin and patted the bulge in his back pants pocket.

"Tory, what about lunch?"

"Six peanut butter sandwiches. Mom made them."

"Steve?"

"Toilet paper," Steve mumbled. "I always get stuck with the toilet paper."

"Your dad runs a supermarket so you get it free," said Lulu and went on. "Gus, did you bring the canteen?"

"Yep. Filled it with grape soda, too," said Gus, and he held up the dented canteen he'd rescued from a trash can.

"Where's Edgar?"

"Making his bed and brushing his teeth," grinned Melvin.

"Here he comes," said Tory, as Edgar shot around the red brick corner waving a yellow fly swatter and nearly running down a pigeon.

"Hi, Lulu. Sorry I'm late."

Lulu nodded. "OK. We're all here. Let's go."

Faded blue jeans and faded, striped T-shirts were already growing warm in the early morning sunlight as Lulu, pigtail bouncing against her back and sheath knife bouncing against her hip, led the gang westward toward the subway.

From the four points of the compass grownup people streamed toward the subway too, on their way to work. It was Monday. Lulu always picked rush hours to ride the subway. She believed very strongly that no kid under 12 should have to pay.

"Now remember," said Lulu as the gang paused at the uptown entrance for the familiar last minute instruction, "look small. Go through with a crowd. And don't everybody go under the same stile. Are you ready?"

"Ready," chorused the gang.

One by one they scattered down the steep flight of stairs and disappeared in the blackness below ground. Once through the turnstile free, each made his way to the head of the platform where the first car of the subway train would stop.

As she stood waiting for the train with the gang

gathered close around her, Lulu wondered at the strange quiet of crowded subway stations.

Then a low, distant rumble that shook the platform turned all the people's heads. Somewhere in the tunnel a subway train raced along the narrow rails. Suddenly, a beam of light flashed from behind a curve, the rumble grew and grew into a mighty roar, and the black train came crashing into the white-tiled station.

People pushed to get off the train. People pushed to get on. The doors slid shut. The car gave a jerk, and the train rumbled out of the station on its way to the next stop.

It was a long ride. The train stopped many times. And after each stop the shoving crowds thinned, until the Eighth Street gang—all except Lulu—sat facing each other, rocking back and forth with the motion of the train. Melvin watched Tory. Tory watched Steve. Steve watched Gus. Gus watched Edgar. And Edgar watched a mean old lady who kept staring at Lulu's knife. Lulu stood in her usual spot at the head of the car. Feet set wide apart, hands

pressed against the wire-meshed glass, Lulu watched the signal lights rush by.

"Two hundred and BLURP Street. Last stop," squawked the intercom.

"Are we there?" asked Edgar.

"Almost," said Lulu. "Just down the stairs and along the highway a little."

It was really hot now. Even when they walked on the sand that bordered the cement highway, the heat cut through their thick-soled sneakers. A field with tall grass, dusty and bent, grew at the edge of the highway. But it got tangled in shoelaces and was hard to walk through. Lulu didn't seem to mind the heat or the walking. Tory began to hum a downbeat tune to her long, swinging stride. Lulu smiled.

"How much longer?" asked Edgar.

"Let's stop for some soda," said Gus.

"Where are you taking us?" asked Melvin.

"It's a surprise," said Lulu. And they all sat down in a ditch by the side of the road and had a swig of warm grape soda.

Crickets trilled in the tall grasses. Cars, buses and

trucks sped by on the highway. And after a short time Lulu got up.

"It's not far," she said. "We're almost there."

"Where?" asked Melvin.

"You'll see," said Lulu over her shoulder, and she struck out across the field toward the woods on the far side.

"Boy," said Melvin, as they tramped into the dense pine woods, "smell all those pine needles."

"It sure is a lot cooler," said Gus.

"This is great," said Tory.

"I'm tired," said Edgar, and he swatted at a little cloud of gnats flying in a shaft of sunlight.

"Hey, come here," called Steve. "Look what I've found. Animal tracks." And the whole gang gathered around Steve and bent over for a closer look.

"They're deer prints," said Lulu.

"Will we see a deer?" asked Steve.

"Maybe," said Lulu. "Mostly you hear deer, and deer see you."

"We're a long way from home," said Edgar. "I don't like bugs."

17

"You don't like anything," snapped Melvin. And everyone fell silent as they padded single file along the soft, narrow, tree-lined path. Over a tree root, around a rock, and across a mossy ditch marched the Eighth Street gang.

Suddenly, Lulu stopped short. They had come to a sharp bend in the path.

"OK, everybody. Shut your eyes," said Lulu.

"Oh, cripes," muttered Melvin.

"Come on, gang," urged Lulu. "It's a surprise." So they all shut their eyes, took hands and let Lulu lead them around the bend.

"Now!" said Lulu.

"*WOW!*" said the guys.

Nearby in a tree a blue jay screamed and squirrels rustled for nuts in the underbrush. But no one moved. There, in front of them, stood a tiny tar-paper shack with a sign that read: CLUBHOUSE nailed to the door.

"It's beautiful," said Steve.

"How did it get here?" asked Tory.

"Someone built it," said Melvin.

19

"Who?" asked Gus.

"How do I know," said Melvin.

"I found it," said Lulu. "It's empty. No one lives in it. It's a perfect clubhouse. As soon as we fix it up, we can hold meetings here once a week." And she looked hopefully at the others.

"It's beautiful," said Steve again.

"It's awfully far away," said Edgar. "But nobody else has a clubhouse, do they?"

"Nobody," said Lulu proudly. And she took them through the thick grass clearing and showed them around.

"There's a stream out back and a blackberry patch, too," shouted Melvin from across the clearing.

"Maybe I'll catch some tadpoles and turtles," said Steve.

"First," said Lulu, "we have to wash."

"Wash!" exploded Melvin.

"Yes," said Lulu.

"Right now?" asked Tory.

"Yes," replied Lulu, in a no-nonsense tone.

"I'll just get dirty again," said Gus.

"Aw, what's the difference," said Steve. "Come on, Melvin, let's have the soap."

"Girls," said Melvin in disgust. And he stomped after the others to the back of the shack and down to the stream.

The water in the stream ran cold and fresh, carrying the foam from the soap away over pebbles and sand.

"Legs, too," said Lulu.

"You sound like my mother," said Edgar.

"Girls," Melvin muttered again. But he untied his sneakers, took off his socks and scrubbed. The water did feel nice.

"OK," said Lulu. "Let's fix up the clubhouse."

"When are we going to eat?" asked Gus.

"Never!" said Melvin.

"As soon as we fix up the clubhouse," said Lulu, and she gave Melvin one of her hardest looks.

First they gathered together a bundle of twigs. And Lulu showed them how the Indians used the twigs to sweep their tepees. Cobwebs and dead flies, weeds and pebbles—all flew before Steve's crazy sweeping. Not a speck of dust was left in the shack. Even the hard dirt floor was spotless.

21

Next they hunted for some sawed-up logs to sit on and a large flat stone to use for a table. Edgar found some pieces of charcoal; good for drawing pictures on the walls like the cavemen did, he said. And Lulu picked some blackberries and arranged them in six large leaf-cups.

At last the clubhouse was ready. The Eighth Street gang filed through the narrow, wooden doorway and took their seats around the large stone table. There were only five places. Lulu came in last.

"Hey, Lulu," said Melvin, before she had cleared the door, "there's no more grape soda left. How about filling the canteen with water?"

"OK," said Lulu. And, taking the canteen, she headed toward a wider, faster-flowing part of the stream.

The sun told her it was way past lunchtime, and as she watched the air bubbles escape from the submerged canteen, she thought hungrily about the peanut butter sandwich and the blackberries waiting for her back at the clubhouse. She rinsed the canteen twice. Then, when it had filled again, she screwed on the top and started back to the shack.

Halfway there, she paused and listened. The day

had grown suddenly very quiet. The hum of insects had stopped. Animal noises had stopped. And not a sound came from the tar-paper shack.

"It's too quiet," said Lulu out loud and, looking up at the sky, she added, "Wonder if a storm's coming?" Then putting both thoughts from her mind, she rounded the shack and faced the door. The sign read,

CLUBHOUSE
No Girls Allowed

Lulu stared at the black scrawled sign. One second. Two seconds. She felt her eyes begin to smart and her jaws clamp shut. Every part of her ached to fight. She wanted to scream, to break down the door. Most of all, she wanted to get at that Melvin and fix him good.

Instead, Lulu turned tail and ran. Like some wild animal, she ran and ran. Back the way they had come. Back to the open field, where a tangle of dried grass caught her ankle and sent her sprawling.

She lay there a moment trying to catch her breath, trying not to cry. But it was hopeless. From deep in-

side came a great shuddering sob. Then another. And another. There were no other sounds in the field, just the sound of her sobbing.

When there was no more crying left inside her, Lulu stopped. She sat up, blew her nose on a corner of her T-shirt, took a drink from the canteen, then did some thinking. And peace and quiet and cricket noises returned to the late-afternoon field.

It was while she sat in the tall grass thinking what to do next, that the idea popped out of nowhere right into her head. *Pop!*

"Man, oh man," whispered Lulu, and a wide grin split her face. "They don't know how to get home! They're stuck here without me!" The more she thought about it, the funnier it got. Until Lulu found herself rocking back and forth, and laughing and laughing as hard as she had cried.

"Wait'll that Melvin finds out I've gone. Taken off!" shouted Lulu across the field, and doubled up in new gales of laughter. "I've got to go back . . . oh . . ." she groaned, holding her sides, "and see ol' Melvin get his." And she picked up the canteen, slung it over her shoulder and headed in a roundabout way back to the shack.

There was no more sun left in the woods when Lulu reached the clearing. Going on all fours, she scrambled up the back of a cluster of boulders that overlooked the shack, and settled herself down in a rocky nest to wait.

The clubhouse door was still shut tight, the sign still on the door. And now daylight was beginning to fade. Lulu could feel the air growing cooler up where she sat, high among the rocks. And as she sat there waiting, so heavy a hush fell upon the woods that the snapping of the smallest twig cracked like a gunshot in the quiet. Lulu began to shiver. The suspense of waiting grew and grew until all she could hear was the beating of her heart.

Lulu looked down to brush an ant off her leg. When she looked up, the clubhouse door was ajar and there was Gus, poking his head out, taking a quick look around.

"She's not here," he said, and shut the door again.

Lulu grinned.

In a few minutes, the door swung wide open and out stepped Tory. He looked behind the right corner

of the shack. He looked behind the left corner of the shack.

"Honest, she's not here," he said.

"She's gotta be here," shouted a voice. And out came Melvin, like an angry bull. Steve followed close on his heels.

"Lu-lu . . . Lulu?" called Steve. "You see," he said, turning to Melvin, "she's not here."

28

"My mom'll kill me if I'm not home at 7," said
Edgar, and he leaned heavily against the door frame.

"Then you're already dead," said Melvin.

"But what are we gonna do?" asked Gus.

"Let me think. Let me think," said Melvin. So they sat down in a circle and waited for Melvin to think.

"You really got us into a mess, this time," sighed Steve.

"You and your great ideas," muttered Tory.

"I wish you were Lulu, then I'd be home eating supper," said Gus.

"You really aren't so smart, after all," piped up Edgar.

"OK! OK!" grumbled Melvin. Then after a moment, he added softly, "I don't feel so good . . . I wish Lulu were here."

"I *am* here," said Lulu. And she walked triumphantly into the clearing.

There was a long, silent staring match. Lulu stood facing Melvin. Melvin sat sullen and glaring. Then he ducked his head. "OK. OK. It was just a joke anyway," he said. "Where's the charcoal?"

"Here," said Edgar.

Melvin took the charcoal and the sign and went inside the shack.

"Hi, Lulu," said Steve. "I saved you some blackberries."

"Thank you," said Lulu. "You don't have to bring the toilet paper back to the city. You can leave it here for next time."

"I'm glad you're here," said Edgar.

"Me, too," said Lulu.

And Melvin came out of the shack, closed the door and pushed the sign back onto the nail.

CLUBHOUSE
No Girls Allowed
EXCEPT Lulu

"OK?" asked Melvin.

"OK," said Lulu. "Let's go home." And she took her place at the head of the small column and led the Eighth Street gang out of the woods.

It was a very quiet trip. They made only one stop at the deer print.

"See that?" said Lulu, pointing to a clump of shiny, reddish-green leaves. *"That's* poison ivy. That's why we washed."